Eagle  Eyes

A CHILD'S GUIDE TO PAYING ATTENTION

Eagle  Eyes

A CHILD'S GUIDE TO PAYING ATTENTION

BY JEANNE GEHRET, M.A.
Illustrations and design by Susan Covert

Verbal Images Press
Fairport, New York

Steven McFann

Many thanks to those who reviewed and consulted on this book:

Cheryl Guenther, parent, The Norman Howard School, New York; **Corinne Olson,** student, New York; **Harvey Parker, Ph.D.,** founder of Children with Attention Deficit Disorders (CH.A.D.D.), Florida; **Jon Price, M.D., F.A.A.P.,** pediatrician, Ohio; **Peg Schoenfeld,** special education teacher, New York; **John F. Taylor, Ph.D.,** family psychologist, Oregon. Special thanks to **Judy Olson,** board member of the Greater Rochester Attention Deficit Disorder Association (GRADDA), who asked for *Eagle Eyes* to be written; and to the naturalists at the Cumming Nature Center of the Rochester Museum and Science Center.

Printed in the United States of America
First printing: October 1990
Second printing: November 1991
Third printing: December 1992
Fourth printing: October 1993
Fifth printing: February 1995
Sixth printing: November 1995

Cataloging-in-Publication Data
Gehret, Jeanne.
    Eagle Eyes : a child's guide to paying attention / by Jeanne Gehret; illustrations by Susan Covert
    Includes bibliographical references.
    SUMMARY: Like a river overflowing its banks, Ben wreaks havoc until he learns to recognize and control his attention deficit disorder.
    ISBN 1-884281-11-7 (pbk.)
    ISBN 1-884281-16-8 (hbk.)
    1. Attention deficit disorders--Juvenile literature. I. Title II. Title: A child's guide to paying attention.
RJ496.A86G4 1991   153.1532   QBI91-1854

Verbal Images Press
19 Fox Hill Drive • Fairport, New York 14450
(716) 377-3807 • Fax (716) 377-5401

When my family goes to Birdsong Trail, I spot more wildlife than anybody else. Our last couple trips there didn't go so well, though. Here's what happened.

  We took birdseed because the chickadees are so tame that they eat right out of people's hands. As soon as I saw the hungry gray birds, I dropped some food on the path. "Ben, stop it," Emily snapped. "If you drop it on the path they won't eat out of our hands." Why didn't I think of that?

As we hiked along the snowy path near the pond, my eyes followed a chickadee to the top of an oak. I spied a clump of leaves and sticks — a nest? An eagle circled high overhead. Suddenly it swooped down into the water and grabbed a fish.

I ran on ahead to where Emily was feeding chickadees. "Emily, guess what," I panted. "I saw an eagle's nest and..." In my haste I tripped, scattering seed on the path. The chickadees flew away from my sister and gathered at my feet, eating greedily.

"You klutz!" she cried. "Can't you ever be quiet? You scared the birds away from me...and now they're all eating at your feet!"

Crying, she turned to Mom and Dad. "I can't have any fun when Ben's around. He's such a pain!" I threw some snow at her.

"Ben, stop!" Mom said. "Would you please be more careful not to scare the birds? Come on, Emily; we'll find other chickadees around the bend."

A pain, I thought—that's me. Always ruining things, making people mad. I stayed behind, thinking, *They're better off without me.*

I walked so slowly that I must have examined every inch of that trail—the bird feeder where cardinals feast, the deer footprints by the bridge, the signpost with the eagle painted on it. I wanted to tell Emily what I saw, but she was still mad. She glared at me all the way home.

After supper Mom said, "Time for homework, kids. Go get your folders and let's see what you have to do."

Emily spoke up quickly. "I don't have any. I finished mine in school on Friday."

"Good job, honey. How about you, Ben?"

"I don't have any either," I replied. But a few minutes later she returned holding a note from my folder. Frowning, she read, "Benjamin has not done his homework for two days. Please have him complete pages 67-75 of these worksheets."

So I had to sit and work the rest of the evening while Emily got to rearrange her fish tank. I was so angry I couldn't fall asleep until midnight.

"Pass your homework in, class," my teacher said the next morning. I smiled to myself, glad that I had mine in my folder for a change. But no, my folder was empty! After all that work!

Shortly after that, Dad took me to see Dr. Lawson. She told me I have Attention Deficit Disorder, which is often called ADD for short. ADD means that my body doesn't have enough of the chemicals that help me control how I move and think. I forget to take my homework to school because my thoughts run ahead of me. That's why I bump into things, too. And all that energy keeps me awake into the night.

All this time I thought I was nothing but a clumsy, bad kid. Huh!

Dad explained that I have eagle eyes; I notice everything. But eagles know when to stop looking around and zoom in on their prey. Me, I just keep noticing more things and miss my catch.

susan covert

Dr. Lawson showed Dad and me some tricks so I can pay attention to what's important. That night we made up a song about getting ready for school so I'll have everything I need. Here's how it goes:

The Morning Song

adapted from the traditional tune "Oats, peas, beans, and barley"

1. Clothes, hair, shoes, and backpack, lunch, Clothes, hair, shoes and
2. Clear the ta- ble wash my face, Get my coat and

1. backpack, lunch, Clothes, hair, shoes and backpack, lunch, That is what I do.
2. get my boots, Grab my backpack, give a kiss, That is what I do.

When I sing "backpack," I know it's time to put my homework in my backpack. Since I've started singing the Morning Song, I haven't forgotten any of my school things.

Another thing I like is the soft music that Mom gave me to help me relax at night. It quiets the thoughts that run around inside my head. Dr. Lawson prescribed medicine that gives my body more of the chemicals it needs.

Dr. Lawson also taught us to play the Feelings Game. Dad makes a face like he's angry, or sad, or pleased, and I guess how he's feeling by reading his face and body. One day, when I was crayoning on Emily's homework, I noticed that her face looked like Daddy's does when he's mad. I stopped right away and she didn't go crying to Mom like she usually does.

Since we've been doing the things Dr. Lawson suggested, I feel better. And I don't feel like I'm such a pain in the neck. In fact, people even seem glad to have me around.

This spring, when Dad and Emily and I returned to Birdsong Trail, I took binoculars to watch for eagles. Instead, I spied a pair of ducks in the stream.

A thunderstorm sent us dashing back toward the car. Just as we were rounding the bend by the bird feeder, thunder clapped and lightning nearly blinded us. Dad tripped over a rock and twisted his knee.

His face wrinkled with pain. "Emily, you're the oldest," he said. "Will you follow the trail back to the ranger station and get help?" She looked scared. "I don't know the way...." she began.

"I can find it, Dad!" I interrupted. "After you pass the old gate, you follow this trail till you cross the creek and turn at the signpost with the eagle on it. It's not far to the ranger station after that."

"Ben, I knew those eagle eyes of yours would come in handy," Dad replied. "You'll find the way just fine. Emily can stay here to keep me company."

As I turned to go, Dad called, "Hurry, Ben! I need you."

Swift as an eagle, I zoomed off toward the ranger station and got help for Dad. I was the only one who could do it.

And that's when I realized it's good to be me.

PARENT RESOURCE GUIDE

Personal Glimpses

I awoke from a heart-pounding nightmare. In the dream I stood watching my first-grade son climb on the balcony above. "Get down or you'll fall!" I cried, just before he tumbled over. I caught him one instant before he would have cracked his head on the flagstone.

In the cool light of morning, I sought the meaning of this dream. The previous year our kindergartner Daniel had been diagnosed with Attention Deficit Disorder (ADD) and learning disabilities (LD). The psychologist's recommendations for changes at home and school had worked almost immediately. But when Dan started first grade in a new school, his teacher and principal refused to accept the diagnosis or make necessary modifications. By November, Dan was teetering on the edge of failure and hating himself for causing trouble.

My dream sounded a clear alarm: our son was falling fast! But if I moved quickly, I could save him.

To provide the safety net Dan needed, my husband and I called upon our area support groups for ADD and LD. These compassionate friends showed us other youngsters in similar danger of smashing themselves on the rocky trail of ADD. Writing *Eagle Eyes* empowered me to share some of the advice that helped us survive this dangerous, but sometimes-exhilarating, journey.

Like Ben in *Eagle Eyes,* many youngsters with ADD become overloaded with all the sights and sounds that compete for their attention. Hyperactive children compensate by attending to everything; under-active ones focus so intently on one thing that they fail to notice other stimuli, even important ones. Often this over- or under-focusing gets them into trouble; but sometimes it adds an exciting, valuable dimension to living.

Once we identify their problem, how can we help? Consider this modern parable:

> *Sarah and three classmates were designated as photographers during a field trip to a farm. Three of the young photojournalists used point-and-shoot cameras with no adjustments. But Sarah brought a complicated camera with two different lenses for far-off scenery and for close-ups.*
>
> *When all the photos were mounted the following week, the students admired the sharply-focused images of friends boarding the bus, petting the animals, and drinking fresh cider. These were taken by the three students with non-adjustable cameras. No one, however, could figure out where or why Sarah*

had taken the pictures she displayed. One portrayed the entire mountain behind the farm, while the other recorded the detailed image of a tire tread in the mud. Her other pictures stayed home; they were out of focus.

When Sarah's classmates began making fun of her, two teachers brainstormed how to help.

"Sarah can't handle such sophisticated equipment," said Gerry, the first teacher. "She should use a fixed-focus camera so she can take fun snapshots like everyone else. Then she'll fit in better."

"But Sarah has the makings of a great photographer," objected Pat, the second teacher. "She needs those fancy lenses to translate her vision into reality. I say let her keep the complicated camera."

"Let's do both," said Gerry. "I'll take Sarah aside and explain that her gear is different. By mastering it, she can produce really special pictures. You show her how to take the casual snapshots with a regular lens, so she can fit in with the other kids. Then I'll teach her how to use the other lenses to take those unusual pictures she likes."

Sarah became the official class photographer, shooting every kind of picture that anyone could possibly want. Her classmates were so happy with her snapshots of them that they grew to enjoy her artistic photos, too.

Just as Sarah has a more complex camera than her classmates, so youngsters with ADD have more complicated neurological equipment. If used properly, their brains can often accomplish more than others. But ADD children will seldom produce "normal" results unless they are taught specifically how to adapt; like Sarah, they have so many options to choose from!

How can we best help them? Teach them to conform when necessary, but encourage them to explore their special gifts, too. Such acceptance forms a safety net for youngsters who risk bringing new perspectives to our conventional world.

PARENT RESOURCE GUIDE

New Vistas on Attention Deficit Disorder (ADD)

In November 1990, parents of children with ADD heaved a collective sigh of relief when Dr. Alan Zametkin released a report that hyperactivity (which is closely linked to ADD) results from an insufficient rate of glucose metabolism in the brain. Finally, commented a supporter, we have an answer to skeptics who pass this off as bratty behavior caused by poor parenting.

We parents have no choice but to deal with our youngsters' ADD, because their behaviors cry out to us for a response. Each time we see a typical ADD problem—losing personal belongings, speaking out of turn, or failing to follow through on responsibilities—we have to make a choice about our reaction. Do we diminish our children with angry criticism or work with them so the situations don't arise again?

Here are several things our family has done to help life run more smoothly with our ADD child. I hope they work for you, too.

- Learn all you can about how ADD affects people from childhood through adulthood. Read about it; get counseling to identify specific ways your child can adjust; join a support group to swap stories with other parents.

- Restructure your home environment to accommodate your ADD child. She'll be less distracted when you follow a daily schedule, as we do with the "Morning Song" to help our children get ready for school. Reduce the clutter in your child's room by helping her sort belongings into their assigned places. Choose closed boxes rather than open bins and soothing colors instead of busy wallpaper.

- Support your child's teacher by telling her about his strengths and weaknesses and by lending her books or videos on ADD. Ask her to seat him near her desk; to stand next to him when giving directions; to help him keep his workspace organized; and to shorten homework assignments when he becomes overwhelmed (just the odd numbers in math, rather than all the problems, for example). Empty his backpack frequently and follow through on notes he forgets to bring to your attention.

- Consider medication, if recommended by your child's physician. The right prescription can help your ADD youngster settle down long enough to benefit from the other steps I've outlined. However, medication *should never be considered a substitute* for the necessary changes at home and at school, and it must be monitored frequently.

- Experiment with ways to calm your child and help her focus. You can often soothe a youngster who fidgets by rubbing her back softly in a circular motion. (You're effectively fidgeting for her!) If she has trouble going to sleep, let her run a fan or listen to instrumental music designed for meditation and relaxation. A backrub or foot rub before bed can finish the day on a friendly note.

- Schedule regular times for your personal self-renewal, and consider some of the following activities: worship; giving or receiving a massage; meditation and/or yoga; exercise or sports; taking a class; taking a walk or a leisurely bath; going to the library; going on "dates" with a friend or spouse; "adults-only" dinners at home, spending time on your hobby, etc. If you feel guilty about devoting time to yourself, remind yourself that the peace and perspective you gain from such pursuits will spill over into family life and everyone else will benefit, too.

Feel overwhelmed? You probably will be if you try to maintain a "normal" family life that includes hours of TV and a dizzying round of after-school activities, social obligations, and committees. Our family is happier when we concentrate on the essentials—academics and work, family time, and periods of self-renewal. After we've met these needs, we add small doses of the "extras". It's a constant juggling act, but worth the effort. Because of this structure, all of us seem to have a stronger sense of who we are, what we want, and how we're going to get it.

—Jeanne Gehret

A Quick Overview of Attention Deficit Disorder

The Symptoms—With and Without Hyperactivity

Attention Deficit Disorder can be present with or without hyperactivity. The behaviors listed below are commonly attributed to Attention Deficit Disorder with Hyperactivity (ADHD). The affected child will have at least eight of the following characteristics before the age of seven:

- difficulty sitting still; feeling restless
- tendency to get out of classroom seat
- distractibility
- difficulty waiting for a turn
- blurting out answers
- difficulty following instructions
- difficulty paying attention
- switching from one task to another without completing any
- difficulty playing quietly
- talking too much
- interrupting
- losing or forgetting things
- failing to notice how others feel
- doing dangerous things frequently.

When hyperactivity is not present, the primary symptoms are failure to pay attention, difficulty staying organized, and acting quiet or withdrawn. Children who have ADD without hyperactivity are often overlooked because they are not noisy or overactive.

Prevalence Through the Lifespan

Estimates on ADD range from 3 percent to 5 percent of the U.S. population—between 1.4 and 2.2 million.

In about one-third of children with ADD, many symptoms persist into adulthood. Adults with ADD often report that they have trouble establishing and keeping relationships, staying organized, or holding a steady job. They may find it difficult to concentrate for a long time and need frequent changes in their lives. However, adults with ADD often have great success in creative careers that require them to see many perspectives at once; have high energy; perform multiple tasks simultaneously; and launch new projects.

ALSO BY JEANNE GEHRET:

I'm Somebody Too
Eagle Eyes' sister tells how it feels to have a brother with ADD.
Novel for ages 9 and up.

The Don't-give-up Kid and Learning Differences
Explains learning differences from the perspective of a child who has it.
Picture book for ages 6 to 10.

Susan B. Anthony And Justice For All
Biography of the famous reformer who overcame sexism and slavery.
Ages 9 and up.

NEW! ASK ABOUT:

Teacher Handbook on I'm Somebody Too
Reproducible workbook applying the multiple-intelligences approach to
teach reading and writing, acceptance of differences, and more.

Special Reports
Short, concise articles on hard-to-find specifics about the daily
challenges of coping with differences.

 **Verbal Images Press**

19 Fox Hill Drive • Fairport, New York 14450
(716) 377-3807 • Fax (716) 377-5401